'SHE ONLY
WISHED TO PROVE
TO HERSELF SHE
WAS ONCE
MORE ON A
TRAIN GOING
SOMEWHERE.'

KATHERINE ANNE PORTER
Born 1890, Indian Creek, Texas, USA
Died 1980, Silver Spring, Maryland, USA

'The Cracked Looking-Glass' was originally published in 1932
and appears in the collection *Pale Horse, Pale Rider*.

PORTER IN PENGUIN MODERN CLASSICS
*Pale Horse, Pale Rider*

# KATHERINE ANNE PORTER

## *The Cracked Looking-Glass*

PENGUIN BOOKS

PENGUIN CLASSICS

UK | USA | Canada | Ireland | Australia
India | New Zealand | South Africa

Penguin Books is part of the Penguin Random House group
of companies whose addresses can be found at global.
penguinrandomhouse.com.

Penguin
Random House
UK

This edition first published 2018
001

The moral rights of the author have been asserted

Set in 11.2/13.75 pt Dante MT Std
Typeset by Jouve (UK), Milton Keynes
Printed in Great Britain by Clays Ltd, St Ives plc

ISBN: 978–0–241–33962–6

www.greenpenguin.co.uk

MIX
Paper from
responsible sources
FSC® C018179

Penguin Random House is committed to a
sustainable future for our business, our readers
and our planet. This book is made from Forest
Stewardship Council® certified paper.

Dennis heard Rosaleen talking in the kitchen and a man's voice answering. He sat with his hands dangling over his knees, and thought for the hundredth time that sometimes Rosaleen's voice was company to him, and other days he wished all day long she didn't have so much to say about everything. More and more the years put a quietus on a man; there was no earthly sense in saying the same things over and over. Even thinking the same thoughts grew tiresome after a while. But Rosaleen was full of talk as ever. If not to him, to whatever passer-by stopped for a minute, and if nobody stopped, she talked to the cats and to herself. If Dennis came near she merely raised her voice and went on with whatever she was saying, so it was nothing for her to shout suddenly, 'Come out of that, now – how often have I told ye to keep off the table?' and the cats would scatter in all directions with guilty faces. 'It's enough to make a man lep out of his shoes,' Dennis would complain. 'It's not meant for you, darlin',' Rosaleen would say, as if that cured everything, and if he didn't go away at once, she would start some kind of story. But today she kept shooing him out of the place and hadn't a kind word in her mouth, and Dennis in exile felt that everything and everybody was welcome in the place but himself. For the twentieth time he approached on tiptoe and listened at the parlor keyhole.

Rosaleen was saying: 'Maybe his front legs might look a little stuffed for a living cat, but in the picture it's no great matter. I said to Kevin, "You'll never paint that cat alive," but Kevin did it, with house paint mixed in a saucer, and a small brush the way he could put in all them fine lines. His legs look like that because I wanted him pictured on the table, but it wasn't so, he was on my lap the whole time. He was a wonder after the mice, a born hunter bringing them in from morning till night—'

Dennis sat on the sofa in the parlor and thought: 'There it is. There she goes telling it again.' He wondered who the man was, a strange voice, but a loud and ready gabbler as if maybe he was trying to sell something. 'It's a fine painting, Miz O'Toole,' he said, 'and who did you say the artist was?'

'A lad named Kevin, like my own brother he was, who went away to make his fortune,' answered Rosaleen. 'A house painter by trade.'

'The spittin' image of a cat!' roared the voice.

'It is so,' said Rosaleen. 'The Billy-cat to the life. The Nelly-cat here is own sister to him, and the Jimmy-cat and the Annie-cat and the Mickey-cat is nephews and nieces, and there's a great family look between all of them. It was the strangest thing happened to the Billy-cat, Mr Pendleton. He sometimes didn't come in for his supper till after dark, he was so taken up with the hunting, and then one night he didn't come at all, nor the next day neither, nor the next, and me with him on my mind so I didn't get a wink of sleep. Then at midnight on the third night I did go to sleep, and the Billy-cat came into my room and lep upon my pillow and said: "Up beyond the north field there's a maple tree with a great scar where the branch was taken away by the storm, and near to it is a flat stone, and there you'll find me. I was caught in a trap," he says; "wasn't set for me," he says, "but it got me all the same. And now be easy in your mind about me," he says, "for it's all over." Then he went away, giving me a look over his shoulder like a human creature, and I woke up Dennis and told him. Surely as we live, Mr Pendleton, it was all true. So Dennis went beyond the north field and brought him home and we buried him in the garden and cried over him.' Her voice broke and lowered and Dennis shuddered for fear she was going to shed tears before this stranger.

'For God's *sake*, Miz O'Toole,' said the loud-mouthed

man, 'you can't get around that now, can you? Why, that's the most remarkable thing I ever heard!'

Dennis rose, creaking a little, and hobbled around to the east side of the house in time to see a round man with a flabby red face climbing into a rusty old car with a sign painted on the door. 'Always something, now,' he commented, putting his head in at the kitchen door. Always telling a tall tale!'

'Well,' said Rosaleen, without the least shame, 'he wanted a story so I gave him a good one. That's the Irish in me.'

'Always making a thing more than it is,' said Dennis. 'That's the way it goes.'

Rosaleen turned a little edgy. 'Out with ye!' she cried, and the cats never budged a whisker. 'The kitchen's no place for a man! How often must I tell ye?'

'Well, hand me my hat, will you?' said Dennis, for his hat hung on a nail over the calendar and had hung there within easy reach ever since they had lived in the farmhouse. A few minutes later he wanted his pipe, lying on the lamp shelf where he always kept it. Next he had to have his barn boots at once, though he hadn't seen them for a month. At last he thought of something to say, and opened the door a few inches.

'Wherever have I been sitting unmolested for the past ten years?' he asked, looking at his easy chair with the pillow freshly plumped, sideways to the big table. 'And today it's no place for me?'

'If ye grumble ye'll be sorry,' said Rosaleen gayly, 'and now clear out before I hurl something at ye!'

Dennis put his hat on the parlor table and his boots under the sofa, and sat on the front steps and lit his pipe. It would soon be cold weather, and he wished he had his old leather jacket off the hook on the kitchen door. Whatever was Rosaleen up to now? He decided that Rosaleen was always doing the Irish a great wrong by putting her own faults off on them. To be Irish, he felt, was to be like him, a sober, practical, thinking man, a lover of truth. Rosaleen couldn't see it at all. 'It's just your head is like a stone!' she said to him once, pretending she was joking, but she meant it. She had never appreciated him, that was it. And neither had his first wife. Whatever he gave them, they always wanted something else. When he was young and poor his first wife wanted money. And when he was a steady man with money in the bank, his second wife wanted a young man full of life. 'They're all born ingrates one way or another,' he decided, and felt better at once, as if at last he had something solid to stand on. In September a man could get his death sitting on the steps like this, and little she cared! He clacked his teeth together and felt how they didn't fit any more, and his feet and hands seemed tied on him with strings.

All the while Rosaleen didn't look to be a year older. She might almost be doing it to spite him, except that she wasn't the spiteful kind. He'd be bound to say that for her. But she couldn't forget that her girlhood had been a great triumph in Ireland, and she was forever telling him tales about it, and telling them again. This youth of hers was clearer in his mind than his own. He couldn't remember one thing over another that had happened to him. His past lay like a great lump within him; there it was, he knew it all at once, when he thought of it, like a chest a man has packed away, knowing all that is in it without troubling to name or count the objects. All in a lump it had not been an easy life being named Dennis O'Toole in Bristol, England, where he was brought up and worked sooner than he was able at the first jobs he could find. And his English wife had never forgiven him for pulling her up by the roots and bringing her to New York, where his brothers and sisters were, and a better job. All the long years he had been first a waiter and then head waiter in a New York hotel had telescoped in his mind, somehow. It wasn't the best of hotels, to be sure, but still he was head waiter and there was good money in it, enough to buy this farm in Connecticut and have a little steady money coming in, and what more could Rosaleen ask?

He was not unhappy over his first wife's death a few

years after they left England, because they had never really liked each other, and it seemed to him now that even before she was dead he had made up his mind, if she did die, never to marry again. He had held out on this until he was nearly fifty, when he met Rosaleen at a dance in the County Sligo hall far over on East 86th Street. She was a great tall rosy girl, a prize dancer, and the boys were fairly fighting over her. She led him a dance then for two years before she would have him. She said there was nothing against him except he came from Bristol, and the outland Irish had the name of people you couldn't trust. She couldn't say why – it was just a name they had, worse than Dublin people itself. No decent Sligo girl would marry a Dublin man if he was the last man on earth. Dennis didn't believe this, he'd never heard any such thing against the Dubliners; he thought a country girl would lep at the chance to marry a city man whatever. Rosaleen said, 'Maybe,' but he'd see whether she would lep to marry Bristol Irish. She was chambermaid in a rich woman's house, a fiend of darkness if there ever was one, said Rosaleen, and at first Dennis had been uneasy about the whole thing, fearing a young girl who had to work so hard might be marrying an older man for his money, but before the two years were up he had got over that notion.

It wasn't long after they were married Dennis began

almost to wish sometimes he had let one of those strong-armed boys have her, but he had been fond of her, she was a fine good girl, and after she cooled down a little, he knew he could have never done better. The only thing was, he wished it had been Rosaleen he had married that first time in Bristol, and now they'd be settled together, nearer an age. Thirty years was too much difference altogether. But he never said any such thing to Rosaleen. A man owes something to himself. He knocked out his pipe on the foot scraper and felt a real need to go in the kitchen and find a pipe cleaner.

Rosaleen said, 'Come in and welcome!' He stood peering around wondering what she had been making. She warned him: 'I'm off to milk now, and mind ye keep your eyes in your pocket. The cow now – the creature! Pretty soon she'll be jumping the stone walls after the apples, and running wild through the fields roaring, and it's all for another calf only, the poor deceived thing!' Dennis said, 'I don't see what deceit there is in that.' 'Oh, don't you now?' said Rosaleen, and gathered up her milk pails.

The kitchen was warm and Dennis felt at home again. The kettle was simmering for tea, the cats lay curled or sprawled as they chose, and Dennis sat within himself smiling a sunken smile, cleaning his pipe. In the barn Rosaleen looped up her purple gingham skirts and sat with her forehead pressed against the warm, calm side of the cow, drawing two thick streams of milk into the pail. She said to the cow: 'It's no life, no life at all. A man of his years is no comfort to a woman,' and went on with a slow murmur that was not complaining about the things of her life.

She wished sometimes they had never come to Connecticut where there was nobody to talk to but Rooshans and Polacks and Wops no better than Black Protestants when you come right down to it. And the natives were worse even. A picture of her neighbors up the hill came into her mind: a starved-looking woman in a blackish gray dress, and a jaundiced man with red-rimmed eyes, and their mizzle-witted boy. On Sundays they shambled by in their sad old shoes, walking to the meeting-house, but that was all the religion they had, thought Rosaleen, contemptuously. On week days they beat the poor boy and the animals, and fought between themselves. Never a feast-day, nor a bit of bright color in their clothes, nor a Christian look out of their eyes for a living soul. 'It's just living in mortal sin from one day to the next,' said Rosaleen. But it was Dennis getting old that took the heart out of her. And him with the grandest head of hair she had ever seen on a man. A fine man, oh, a fine man Dennis was in those days! Dennis rose before her eyes in his black suit and white gloves, a knowledgeable man who could tell the richest people the right things to order for a good dinner, such a gentleman in his stiff white shirt front, managing the waiters on the one hand and the customers on the other, and making good money at it. And now. No, she couldn't believe it was Dennis any more. Where was Dennis now? And where was Kevin? She was sorry now she had spited Kevin about his girl. It had been all in fun, really, no harm meant. It was strange if you couldn't speak your heart out to a good friend. Kevin had showed her the picture of his girl, like a clap of thunder it came one day when Rosaleen hadn't even heard there was one. She was a waitress in New York, and if ever Rosaleen had laid eyes on a brassy, bold-faced hussy, the kind the boys make jokes about at home, the kind that comes out to New York and goes wrong, this was the one. 'You're never never keeping steady with her, are you?' Rosaleen had cried out and the tears came into her eyes. 'And why not?' asked Kevin, his chin square as a box. 'We've been great now for three years. Who says a word against her says it against me.' And there they were, not exactly quarreling, but not friends for the moment, certainly, with Kevin putting the picture back in his pocket, saying: 'There's the last of it between us. I was greatly wrong to tell ye!'

That night he was packing up his clothes before he went to bed, but came down and sat on the steps with them awhile, and they made it up by saying nothing, as if nothing had happened. 'A man must do something with his life,' Kevin explained. 'There's always a place to be made in the world, and I'm off to New York, or Boston, maybe.' Rosaleen said, 'Write me a letter, don't forget, I'll be waiting.' 'The very day I know where I'll be,' he promised her. They had parted with false wide smiles on their faces, arms around each other to the very gate. There had come a postcard from New York of the Woolworth building, with a word on it: 'This is my hotel. Kevin.' And never another word for these five years. The wretch, the stump! After he had disappeared down the road with his suitcase strapped on his shoulders, Rosaleen had gone back in the house and had looked at herself in the square looking-glass beside the kitchen window. There was a ripple in the glass and a crack across the middle, and it was like seeing your face in water. 'Before God I don't look like that,' she said, hanging it on the nail again. 'If I did, it's no wonder he was leaving. But I don't.' She knew in her heart no good would come of him running off after that common-looking girl; but it was likely he'd find her out soon, and come back, for Kevin was nobody's fool. She waited and watched for Kevin to come back and confess she had been right, and he would say, 'I'm sorry I hurt your feelings over somebody not fit to look at you!' But now it was five years.

She hung a drapery of crochet lace over the frame on the Billy-cat's picture, and propped it up on a small table in the kitchen, and sometimes it gave her an excuse to mention Kevin's name again, though the sound of it was a crack on the eardrums to Dennis. 'Don't speak of him,' said Dennis, more than once. 'He owed it to send us word. It's ingratitude I can't stand.' Whatever was she going to do with Dennis now, she wondered, and sighed heavily into the flank of the cow. It wasn't being a wife at all to wrap a man in flannels like a baby and put hot-water bottles to him. She got up sighing and kicked back the stool. 'There you are now,' she said to the cow.

She couldn't help feeling happy all at once at the sight of the lamp and the fire making everything cozy, and the smell of vanilla reminded her of perfume. She set the table with a white-fringed cloth while Dennis strained the milk.

'Now, Dennis, today's a big day, and we're having a feast for it.'

'Is it All-Saints?' asked Dennis, who never looked at a calendar any more. What's a day, more or less?

'It is not,' said Rosaleen; 'draw up your chair now.'

Dennis made another guess it was Christmas, and Rosaleen said it was a better day than Christmas, even.

'I can't think what,' said Dennis, looking at the glossy baked goose. 'It's nobody's birthday that I mind.'

Rosaleen lifted the cake like a mound of new snow blooming with candles. 'Count them and see what day is this, will you?' she urged him.

Dennis counted them with a waggling forefinger. 'So it is, Rosaleen, so it is.'

They went on bandying words. It had slipped his mind entirely. Rosaleen wanted to know when hadn't it slipped his mind? For all he ever thought of it, they might never have had a wedding day at all. 'That's not so,' said Dennis. 'I mind well I married you. It's the date that slips me.'

'You might as well be English,' said Rosaleen, 'you might just as well.'

She glanced at the clock, and reminded him it was twenty-five years ago that morning at ten o'clock, and tonight the very hour they had sat down to their first married dinner together. Dennis thought maybe it was telling people what to eat and then watching them eat it all those years that had taken away his wish for food. 'You know I can't eat cake,' he said. 'It upsets my stomach.'

Rosaleen felt sure her cake wouldn't upset the stomach of a nursing child. Dennis knew better, any kind of cake sat on him like a stone. While the argument went on, they ate nearly all the goose which fairly melted on the tongue, and finished with wedges of cake and floods of tea, and Dennis had to admit he hadn't felt better in years. He looked at her sitting across the table from him and thought she was a very fine woman, noticed again her red hair and yellow eyelashes and big arms and strong big teeth, and wondered what she thought of him now he was no human good to her. Here he was, all gone, and he had been so for years, and he felt guilt sometimes before Rosaleen, who couldn't always understand how there comes a time when a man is finished, and there is no more to be done that way. Rosaleen poured out two small glasses of homemade cherry brandy.

'I could feel like dancing itself this night, Dennis,' she told him. 'Do you remember the first time we met in Sligo Hall with the band playing?' She gave him another glass of brandy and took one herself and leaned over with her eyes shining as if she was telling him something he had never heard before.

'I remember a boy in Ireland was a great step-dancer, the best, and he was wild about me and I was a devil to him. Now what makes a girl like that, Dennis? He was a fine match, too, all the girls were glad of a chance with him, but I wasn't. He said to me a thousand times, "Rosaleen, why won't ye dance with me just once?" And I'd say, "Ye've plenty to dance with ye without my wasting my time." And so it went for the summer long with him not dancing at all and everybody plaguing the living life out of him, till in the end I danced with him. After-wards he walked home with me and a crowd of them, and there was a heaven full of stars and the dogs barking far off. Then I promised to keep steady with him, and was sorry for it the minute I promised. I was like that. We used to be the whole day getting ready for the dances, washing our hair and curling it and trying on our dresses and trimming them, laughing fit to kill about the boys and making up things to say to them. When my sister Honora was married they took me for the bride, Dennis, with my white dress ruffled to the heels and my hair with a wreath. Everybody drank my health for the belle of the ball, and said I would surely be the next bride. Honora said for me to save my blushes or I'd have none left for my own wedding. She was always jealous, Dennis, she's jealous of me to this day, you know that.'

'Maybe so,' said Dennis.

'There's no maybe about it,' said Rosaleen. 'But we had grand times together when we was little. I mind the time when my great-grandfather was ninety years old on his deathbed. We watched by turns the night—'

'And he was a weary time on it,' said Dennis, to show his interest. He was so sleepy he could hardly hold up his head.

'He was,' said Rosaleen, 'so this night Honora and me was watching, and we was yawning our hearts out of us, for there had been a great ball the night before. Our mother told us, "Feel his feet from time to time, and when you feel the chill rising, you'll know he's near the end. He can't last out the night," she said, "but stay by him." So there we was drinking tea and laughing together in whispers to keep awake, and the old man lying there with his chin propped on the quilt. "Wait a minute," says Honora, and she felt his feet. "They're getting cold," she says, and went on telling me what she had said to Shane at the ball, how he was jealous of Terence and asks her can he trust her out of his sight. And Honora says to Shane, "No, you cannot," and oh, but he was roaring mad with anger! Then Honora stuffs her fist in her mouth to keep down the giggles. I felt great-grandfather's feet and legs and they was like clay to the knees, and I says, "Maybe we'd better call somebody"; but Honora says, "Oh, there's a power of him left to get cold yet!" So we poured out tea and began to comb and braid each other's hair, and fell to whispering our secrets and laughing more. Then Honora put her hand under the quilt and said, "Rosaleen, his stomach's cold, it's gone he must be by now." Then great-grandfather opened the one eye full of rage and says, "It's nothing of the kind, and to hell with ye!" We let out a great scream, and the others came flying in, and Honora cried out, "Oh, he's dead and gone surely, God rest him!" And would you believe it, it was so. He was gone. And while the old women were washing him Honora and me sat down laughing and crying in the one breath . . . and it was six months later to the very day great-grandfather came to me in the dream, the way I told you, and he was still after Honora and me for laughing in the watch. "I've a great mind to thrash ye within an inch of your life," he told me, "only I'm wailing in Purgatory this minute for them last words to ye. Go and have an extra Mass said for the repose of me soul because it's by your misconduct I'm here at all," he says to me. "Get a move on now," he said. "And be damned to ye!"'

'And you woke up in a sweat,' said Dennis, 'and was off to Mass before daybreak.'

Rosaleen nodded her head. 'Ah, Dennis, if I'd set my heart on that boy I need never have left Ireland. And when I think how it all came out with him. With me so far away, him struck on the head and left for dead in a ditch.'

'You dreamed that,' said Dennis.

'Surely I dreamed it, and it is so. When I was crying and crying over him—' Rosaleen was proud of her crying – 'I didn't know then what good luck I would find here.'

Dennis couldn't think what good luck she was talking about.

17

'Let it pass, then,' said Rosaleen. She went to the corner shelves again. 'The man today was selling pipes,' she said, 'and I bought the finest he had.' It was an imitation meerschaum pipe carved with a crested lion glaring out of a jungle and it was as big as a man's fist.

Dennis said, 'You must have paid a pretty penny for that.'

'It doesn't concern ye,' said Rosaleen. 'I wanted to give ye a pipe.'

Dennis said, 'It's grand carving, I wonder if it'll draw at all.' He filled it and lit it and said there wasn't much taste on a new one, for he was tired holding it up.

'It is such a pipe as my father had once,' Rosaleen said to encourage him. 'And in no time it was fit to knock ye off your feet, he said. So it will be a fine pipe some day.'

'And some day I'll be in my tomb,' thought Dennis, bitterly, 'and she'll find a man can keep her quiet.'

When they were in bed Rosaleen took his head on her shoulder. 'Dennis, I could cry for the wink of an eyelash. When I think how happy we were that wedding day.'

'From the way you carried on,' said Dennis, feeling very sly all of a sudden on that brandy, 'I thought different.'

'Go to sleep,' said Rosaleen, prudishly. 'That's no way to talk.'

Dennis's head fell back like a bag of sand on the pillow.

Rosaleen could not sleep, and lay thinking about marriage: not about her own, for once you've given your word there's nothing to think about in it, but all other kinds of marriages, unhappy ones: where the husband drinks, or won't work, or mistreats his wife and the children. Where the wife runs away from home, or spoils the children or neglects them, or turns a perfect strumpet and flirts with other men: where a woman marries a man too young for her, and he feels cheated and strays after other women till it's just a disgrace: or take when a young girl marries an old man, even if he has money she's bound to be disappointed in some way. If Dennis hadn't been such a good man, God knows what might have come out of it. She was lucky. It would break your heart to dwell on it. Her black mood closed down on her and she wanted to walk the floor holding her head and remembering every unhappy thing in the world. She had had nothing but disasters, one after another, and she couldn't get over them, no matter how long ago they happened. Once she had let entirely the wrong man kiss her, she had almost got into bad trouble with him, and even now her heart stopped on her when she thought how near she'd come to being a girl with no character. There was the Billy-cat and his good heart and his sad death, and it was mixed up with the time her father had been knocked down, by a runaway horse, when the drink was in him, and the time when she had to wear mended stockings to a big ball because that sneaky Honora had stolen the only good ones.

She wished now she'd had a dozen children instead of the one that died in two days. This half-forgotten child suddenly lived again in her, she began to weep for him with all the freshness of her first agony; now he would be a fine grown man and the dear love of her heart. The image of him floated before her eyes plain as day, and became Kevin, painting the barn and the pig sty all colors of the rainbow, the brush swinging in his hand like a bell. He would work like a wild man for days and then lie for days under the trees, idle as a tramp. The darling, the darling lad like her own son. A painter by trade was a nice living, but she couldn't bear the thought of him boarding around the country with the heathen Rooshans and Polacks and Wops with their liquor stills and their outlandish lingo. She said as much to Kevin.

'It's not a Christian way to live, and you a good County Sligo boy.'

So Kevin started to make jokes at her like any other Sligo boy. 'I said to myself, that's a County Mayo woman if ever I clapped eyes on one.'

'Hold your tongue,' said Rosaleen softly as a dove. 'You're talking to a Sligo woman as if you didn't know it!'

'Is it so?' said Kevin in great astonishment. 'Well, I'm

glad of the mistake. The Mayo people are too proud for me.'

'And for me, too,' said Rosaleen. 'They beat the world for holding up their chins about nothing.'

'They do so,' said Kevin, 'but the Sligo people have a right to be proud.'

'And you've a right to live in a good Irish house,' said Rosaleen, 'so you'd best come with us.'

'I'd be proud of that as if I came from Mayo,' said Kevin, and he went on slapping paint on Rosaleen's front gate. They stood there smiling at each other, feeling they had agreed enough, it was time to think of how to get the best of each other in the talk from now on. For more than a year they had tried to get the best of each other in the talk, and sometimes it was one and sometimes another, but a gay easy time and such a bubble of joy like a kettle singing. 'You've been a sister to me, Rosaleen, I'll not forget ye while I have breath,' he had said that the last night.

Dennis muttered and snored a little. Rosaleen wanted to mourn about everything at the top of her voice, but it wouldn't do to wake Dennis. He was sleeping like the dead after all that goose.

Rosaleen said, 'Dennis, I dreamed about Kevin in the night. There was a grave, an old one, but with fresh flowers

21

on it, and a name on the headstone cut very clear but as
if it was in another language and I couldn't make it out
some way. You came up then and I said, "Dennis, what
grave is this?" and you answered me, "That's Kevin's
grave, don't you remember? And you put those flowers
there yourself." Then I said, "Well, a grave it is then, and
let's not think of it any more." Now isn't it strange
to think Kevin's been dead all this time and I didn't
know it?'

Dennis said, 'He's not fit to mention, going off as
he did after all our kindness to him, and not a word
from him.'

'It was because he hadn't the power any more,' said
Rosaleen. 'And ye mustn't be down on him now. I was
wrong to put my judgment on him the way I did. Ah,
but to think! Kevin dead and gone, and all these natives
and foreigners living on, with the paint still on their
barns and houses where Kevin put it! It's very bitter.'

Grieving for Kevin, she drifted into thinking of the
natives and foreigners who owned farms all around her.
She was afraid for her life of them, she said, the way they
looked at you out of their heathen faces, the foreigners
bold as brass, the natives sly and mean. 'The way they do
be selling the drink to all, and burning each other in their
beds and splitting each other's heads with axes,' she complained. 'The decent people aren't safe in their houses.'

Yesterday she had seen that native Guy Richards going by wild-drunk again, fit to do any crime. He was a great offense to Rosaleen, with his shaggy mustaches and his shirt in rags till the brawny skin showed through; a shame to the world, staring around with his sneering eyes; living by himself in a shack and having his cronies in for drink until you could hear them shouting at all hours and careering round the countryside like the devils from hell. He would pass by the house driving his bony gray horse at top speed, standing up in the rackety buggy singing in a voice like a power of scrap-iron falling, drunk as a lord before breakfast. Once when Rosaleen was standing in her doorway, wearing a green checkerboard dress, he yelled at her: 'Hey, Rosie, want to come for a ride?'

'The bold stump!' said Rosaleen to Dennis. 'If ever he lays a finger on me I'll shoot him dead.'

'If you mind your business by day,' said Dennis in a shriveled voice, 'and bar the doors well by night, there'll be no call to shoot anybody.'

'Little you know!' said Rosaleen. She had a series of visions of Richards laying a finger on her and herself shooting him dead in his tracks. 'Whatever would I do without ye, Dennis?' she asked him that night, as they sat on the steps in a soft darkness full of fireflies and the sound of crickets. 'When I think of all the kinds of men there are in the world. That Richards!'

'When a man is young he likes his fun,' said Dennis, amiably, beginning to yawn.

'Young, is it?' said Rosaleen, warm with anger. 'The old crow! Fit to have children grown he is, the same as myself, and I'm a settled woman over her nonsense!'

Dennis almost said, 'I'll never call you old,' but all at once he was irritable too. 'Will you stop your gossiping?' he asked censoriously.

Rosaleen sat silent, without rancor, but there was no denying the old man was getting old, old. He got up as if he gathered his bones in his arms, and carried himself in the house. Somewhere inside of him there must be Dennis, but where? 'The world is a wilderness,' she informed the crickets and frogs and fireflies.

Richards never had offered to lay a finger on Rosaleen, but now and again he pulled up at the gate when he was not quite drunk, and sat with them afternoons on the doorstep, and there were signs in him of a nice-behaved man before the drink got him down. He would tell them stories of his life, and what a desperate wild fellow he had been, all in all. Not when he was a boy, though. As long as his mother lived he had never done a thing to hurt her feelings. She wasn't what you might call a rugged woman, the least thing made her sick, and she was so religious she prayed all day long under her breath at her work, and even while she ate. He had belonged to a society called The Sons of Temperance, with all the boys in the countryside banded together under a vow never to touch strong drink in any form: 'Not even for medicinal purposes,' he would quote, raising his right arm and staring solemnly before him. Quite often he would burst into a rousing march tune which he remembered from the weekly singings they had held: 'With flags of temperance flying, With banners white as snow,' and he could still repeat almost word for word the favorite poem he had been called upon to recite at every meeting: 'At midnight, in his guarded tent, The Turk lay dreaming of the hour—'

Rosaleen wanted to interrupt sometimes and tell him that had been no sort of life, he should have been young in Ireland. But she wouldn't say it. She sat stiffly beside Dennis and looked at Richards severely out of the corner of her eye, wondering if he remembered that time he had yelled 'Hey, Rosie!' at her. It was enough to make a woman wild not to find a word in her mouth for such boldness. The cheek of him, pretending nothing had happened. One day she was racking her mind for some saying that would put him in his place, while he was telling about the clambakes his gang was always having down by the creek behind the rock pile, with a keg of home-brew beer; and the dances the Railroad Street outfit gave every Saturday night in Winston. 'We're always up to some devilment,' he said, looking straight at Rosaleen, and before she could say scat, the hellion had winked his near eye at her. She turned away with her mouth down at the corners; after a long minute, she said, 'Good day to ye, Mr Richards,' cold as ice, and went in the house. She took down the looking-glass to see what kind of look she had on her, but the wavy place made her eyes broad and blurred as the palm of her hands, and she couldn't tell her nose from her mouth in the cracked seam . . .

The pipe salesman came back next month and brought a patent cooking pot that cooked vegetables perfectly without any water in them. 'It's a lot healthier way of cooking, Miz O'Toole,' Dennis heard his mouthy voice going thirteen to the dozen. 'I'm telling you as a friend because you're a good customer of mine.'

'Is it so?' thought Dennis, and his gall stirred within him.

'You'll find it's going to be a perfect godsend for your husband's health. Old folks need to be mighty careful what they eat, and you know better than I do, Miz O'Toole, that health begins or ends right in the kitchen. Now your husband don't look as stout as he might. It's because, tasty as your cooking is, you've been pouring all the good vitamins, the sunlit life-giving elements, right down the sink ... Right down the sink, Miz O'Toole, is where you're pouring your husband's health and your own. And I say it's a shame, a good-looking woman like you wasting your time and strength standing over a cook-stove when all you've got to do from now on is just fill this scientific little contrivance with whatever you've planned for dinner and then go away and read a good book in your parlor while it's cooking – or curl your hair.'

'My hair curls by nature,' said Rosaleen. Dennis almost groaned aloud from his hiding-place.

'For the love of – why, Miz O'Toole, you don't mean to tell me that! When I first saw that hair, I said to myself, why, it's so perfect it looks to be artificial! I was just getting ready to ask you how you did it so I could tell my wife. Well, if your hair curls like that, without any vitamins at all, I want to come back and have a look at it after you've been cooking in this little pot for two weeks.'

Rosaleen said, 'Well, it's not my looks I'm thinking about. But my husband isn't up to himself, and that's the truth, Mr Pendleton. Ah, it would have done your heart good to see that man in his younger days! Strong as an ox he was, the way no man dared to rouse his anger. I've seen my husband, many's the time, swing on a man with his fist and send him sprawling twenty feet, and that for the least thing, mind you! But Dennis could never hold his grudge for long, and the next instant you'd see him picking the man up and dusting him off like a brother and saying, "Now think no more of that." He was too forgiving always. It was his great fault.'

'And look at him now,' said Mr Pendleton, sadly.

Dennis felt pretty hot around the ears. He stood forward at the corner of the house, listening. He had never weighed more than one hundred thirty pounds at his most, a tall thin man he had been always, a little proud of his elegant shape, and not since he left school in Bristol had he lifted his hand in anger against a creature, brute or human. 'He was a fine man a woman could rely on, Mr Pendleton,' said Rosaleen, 'and quick as a tiger with his fists.'

'I might be dead and moldering away to dust the way she talks,' thought Dennis, 'and there she is throwing away the money as if she was already a gay widow woman.' He tottered out, bent on speaking his mind and putting a stop to such foolishness. The salesman turned a floppy smile and shrewd little eyes upon him. 'Hello, Mr O'Toole,' he said, with the manly cordiality he used for husbands. 'I'm just leaving you a little birthday present with the Missis here.'

'It's not my birthday,' said Dennis, sour as a lemon.

'That's just a manner of speaking!' interrupted

Rosaleen, merrily. 'And now many thanks to ye, Mr Pendleton.'

'Many thanks to *you*, Miz O'Toole,' answered the salesman, folding away nine dollars of good green money. No more was said except good day, and Rosaleen stood shading her eyes to watch the Ford walloping off down the hummocky lane. 'That's a nice, decent family man,' she told Dennis, as if rebuking his evil thoughts. 'He travels out of New York, and he always has the latest thing and the best. He's full of admiration for ye, too, Dennis. He said he couldn't call to mind another man of your age as sound as you are.'

'I heard him,' said Dennis. 'I know all he said.'

'Well, then,' said Rosaleen, serenely, 'there's no good saying it over.' She hurried to wash potatoes to cook in the pot that made the hair curl.

The winter piled in upon them, and the snow was shot through with blizzards. Dennis couldn't bear a breath of cold, and all but sat in the oven, rheumy and grunty, with his muffler on. Rosaleen began to feel as if she couldn't bear her clothes on her in the hot kitchen, and when she did the barn work she had one chill after another. She complained that her hands were gnawed to the bone with the cold. Did Dennis realize that now, or was he going to sit like a log all winter, and where was the lad he had promised her to help with the outside work?

Dennis sat wordless under her unreasonableness, thinking she had very little work for a strong-bodied woman, and the truth was she was blaming him for something he couldn't help. Still she said nothing he could take hold of, only nipping his head off when the kettle dried up or the fire went low. There would come a day when she would say outright, 'It's no life here, I won't stay here any longer,' and she would drag him back to a flat in New York, or even leave him, maybe. Would she? Would she do such a thing? Such a thought had never occurred to him before. He peered at her as if he watched her through a keyhole. He tried to think of something to ease her mind, but no plan came. She would look at some harmless thing around the house, say – the calendar, and suddenly tear it off the wall and stuff it in the fire. 'I hate the very sight of it,' she would explain, and she was always hating the very sight of one thing or another, even the cow; almost, but not quite, the cats.

One morning she sat up very tired and forlorn, and began almost before Dennis could get an eye open: 'I had a dream in the night that my sister Honora was sick and dying in her bed, and was calling for me.' She bowed her head on her hands and breathed brokenly to her very toes, and said, 'It's only natural I must go to Boston to find out for myself how it is, isn't it?'

Dennis, pulling on his chest protector she had knitted him for Christmas, said, 'I suppose so. It looks that way.'

Over the coffee pot she began making her plans. 'I could go if only I had a coat. It should be a fur one against this weather. A coat is what I've needed all these years. If I had a coat I'd go this very day.'

'You've a greatcoat with fur on it,' said Dennis.

'A rag of a coat!' cried Rosaleen. 'And I won't have Honora see me in it. She was jealous always, Dennis, she'd be glad to see me without a coat.'

'If she's sick and dying maybe she won't notice,' said Dennis.

Rosaleen agreed. 'And maybe it will be better to buy one there, or in New York – something in the new style.'

'It's long out of your way by New York,' said Dennis. 'There's shorter ways to Boston than that.'

'It's by New York I'm going, because the trains are better,' said Rosaleen, 'and I want to go that way.' There was a look on her face as if you could put her on the rack and she wouldn't yield. Dennis kept silence.

When the postman passed she asked him to leave word with the native family up the hill to send their lad down for a few days to help with the chores, at the same pay as before. And tomorrow morning, if it was all the same to him, she'd be driving in with him to the train. All day long, with her hair in curl papers, she worked getting her things together in the lazy old canvas bag. She put a ham on to bake and set bread and filled the closet off the kitchen with firewood. 'Maybe there'll come a message saying Honora's better and I sha'n't have to go,' she said several times, but her eyes were excited and she walked about so briskly the floor shook.

Late in the afternoon Guy Richards knocked, and floundered in stamping his big boots. He was almost sober, but he wasn't going to be for long. Rosaleen said, 'I've sad news about my sister, she's on her deathbed maybe and I'm going to Boston.'

'I hope it's nothing serious, Missis O'Toole,' said Richards. 'Let's drink her health in this,' and he took out a bottle half full of desperate-looking drink. Dennis said he didn't mind. Richards said, 'Will the lady join us?' and his eyes had the devil in them if Rosaleen had ever seen it.

'I will not,' she said. 'I've something better to do.'

While they drank she sat fixing the hem of her dress, and began to tell again about the persons without number she'd known who came back from the dead to bring word about themselves, and Dennis himself would back her up in it. She told again the story of the Billy-cat, her voice warm and broken with the threat of tears.

Dennis swallowed his drink, leaned over and began to

fumble with his shoelace, his face sunken to a handful of wrinkles, and thought right out plainly to himself: 'There's not a word of truth in it, not a word. And she'll go on telling it to the world's end for God's truth.' He felt helpless, as if he were involved in some disgraceful fraud. He wanted to speak up once for all and say, 'It's a lie, Rosaleen, it's something you've made up, and now let's hear no more about it.' But Richards, sitting there with his ears lengthened, stopped the words in Dennis's throat. The moment passed. Rosaleen said solemnly, 'My dreams never renege on me, Mr Richards. They're all I have to go by.' 'It never happened at all,' said Dennis inside himself, stubbornly. 'Only the Billy-cat got caught in a trap and I buried him.' Could this really have been all? He had a nightmarish feeling that somewhere just out of his reach lay the truth about it, he couldn't swear for certain, yet he was *almost* willing to swear that this had been all. Richards got up saying he had to be getting on to a shindig at Winston. 'I'll take you to the train tomorrow, Missis O'Toole,' he said. 'I love doing a good turn for the ladies.'

Rosaleen said very stiffly, 'I'll be going in with the letter-carrier, and many thanks just the same.'

She tucked Dennis into bed with great tenderness and sat by him a few minutes, putting cold cream on her face. 'It won't be for long,' she told him, 'and you're well taken care of the whole time. Maybe by the grace of God I'll find her recovered.'

'Maybe she's not sick at all,' Dennis wanted to say, and said instead, 'I hope so.' It was nothing to him. Everything else aside, it seemed a great fuss to be making over Honora, who might die when she liked for all Dennis would turn a hair.

Dennis hoped until the last minute that Rosaleen would come to her senses and give up the trip, but at the last minute there she was with her hat and the rag of a coat, a streak of pink powder on her chin, pulling on her tan gloves that smelt of naphtha, flourishing a handkerchief that smelt of Azurea, and going every minute to the window, looking for the postman. 'In this snow maybe he'll be late,' she said in a trembling voice. 'What if he didn't come at all?' She took a last glimpse at herself in the mirror. 'One thing I must remember, Dennis,' she said in another tone. 'And that is, to bring back a looking-glass that won't make my face look like a monster's.'

'It's a good enough glass,' said Dennis, 'without throwing away money.'

The postman came only a few minutes late. Dennis kissed Rosaleen good-by and shut the kitchen door so he could not see her climbing into the car, but he heard her laughing.

'It's just a born liar she is,' Dennis said to himself,

sitting by the stove, and at once he felt he had leaped head-first into a very dark pit. His better self tried to argue it out with him. 'Have you no shame,' said Dennis's better self, 'thinking such thoughts about your own wife?' The baser Dennis persisted. 'It's not half she deserves,' he answered sternly, 'leaving me here by my lone, and for what?' That was the great question. Certainly not to run after Honora, living or dying or dead. Where then? For what on earth? Here he stopped thinking altogether. There wasn't a spark in his mind. He had a lump on his chest that could surely be pneumonia if he had a cold, which he hadn't, specially. His feet ached until you'd swear it was rheumatism, only he never had it. Still, he wasn't thinking. He stayed in this condition for two days, and the under-witted lad from the native farm above did all the work, even to washing the dishes. Dennis ate pretty well, considering the grief he was under.

Rosaleen settled back in the plush seat and thought how she had always been a great traveler. A train was like home to her, with all the other people sitting near, and the smell of newspapers and some kind of nice-smelling furniture polish and the perfume from fur collars, and the train dust and something over and above she couldn't place, but it was the smell of travel: fruit, maybe, or was it machinery? She bought chocolate bars, though she wasn't hungry, and a magazine of love stories, though she was never one for reading. She only wished to prove to herself she was once more on a train going somewhere.

She watched the people coming on or leaving at the stations, greeting, or kissing good-by, and it seemed a lucky sign she did not see a sad face anywhere. There was a cold sweet sunshine on the snow, and the city people didn't look all frozen and bundled up. Their faces looked smooth after the gnarled raw frost-bitten country faces. The Grand Central hadn't changed at all, with all the crowds whirling in every direction, and a noise that almost had a tune in it, it was so steady. She held on to her bag the colored men were trying to get away from her, and stood on the sidewalk trying to remember which direction was Broadway where the moving pictures were. She hadn't seen one for five years, it was high time now! She wished she had an hour to visit her old flat in 164th Street – just a turn around the block would be enough, but there wasn't time. An old resentment rose against Honora, who was a born spoil-sport and would spoil this trip for her if she could. She walked on, getting her directions, brooding a little because she had been such a city girl once, thinking only of dress and a good time, and now she hardly knew one street from another. She went into the first moving-picture theater she saw because she liked the name of it. 'The Prince of Love,' she said to herself. It was about two beautiful young things, a boy with black wavy hair and a girl with curly golden hair, who loved each other and had great troubles, but it all came well in the end, and all the time it was just one fine ballroom or garden after another, and such beautiful clothes! She sniffled a little in the Azurea-smelling handkerchief, and ate her chocolates, and reminded herself these two were really alive and looked just like that, but it was hard to believe living beings could be so beautiful.

After the dancing warm lights of the screen the street was cold and dark and ugly, with the slush and the roar and the millions of people all going somewhere in a great rush, but not one face she knew. She decided to go to Boston by boat the way she used in the old days when she visited Honora. She gazed into the shop windows thinking how the styles in underthings had changed till she could hardly believe her eyes, wondering what Dennis would say if she bought the green glove silk slip with the tea-colored lace. Ah, was he eating his ham now as she told him, and did the boy come to help as he had promised?

She ate ice cream with strawberry preserves on it, and bought a powder puff and decided there was time for another moving picture. It was called 'The Lover King,' and it was about a king in a disguise, a lovely young man with black wavy hair and eyes that would melt in his head, who married a poor country girl who was more beautiful than all the princesses and ladies in the land. Music came out of the screen, and voices talking, and Rosaleen cried, for the love songs went to her heart like a dagger.

Afterward there was just time to ride in a taxi to Christopher Street and catch the boat. She felt happier the minute she set foot on board, how she always loved a ship! She ate her supper thinking, 'That boy didn't have much style to his waiting. Dennis would never have kept him on in the hotel'; and afterward sat in the lounge and listened to the radio until she almost fell asleep there before everybody. She stretched out in her narrow bunk and felt the engine pounding under her, and the grand steady beat shook the very marrow of her bones. The fog horn howled and bellowed through the darkness over the rush of water, and Rosaleen turned on her side. 'Howl for me, that's the way I could cry in the nighttime in that lost heathen place,' for Connecticut seemed a thousand miles and a hundred years away by now. She fell asleep and had no dreams at all.

In the morning she felt this was a lucky sign. At Providence she took the train again, and as the meeting with Honora came nearer, she grew sunken and tired. 'Always

Honora making trouble,' she thought, standing outside the station holding her bag and thinking it strange she hadn't remembered what a dreary ugly place Boston was; she couldn't remember any good times there. Taxi-cab drivers were yelling in her face. Maybe it would be a good thing to go to a church and light a candle for Honora. The taxi scampered through winding streets to the nearest church, with Rosaleen thinking, what she wouldn't give to be able to ride around all day, and never walk at all!

She knelt near the high altar, and something surged up in her heart and pushed the tears out of her eyes. Prayers began to tumble over each other on her lips. How long it had been since she had seen the church as it should be, dressed for a feast with candles and flowers, smelling of incense and wax. The little doleful church in Winston, now who could really pray in it? 'Have mercy on us,' said Rosaleen, calling on fifty saints at once; 'I confess . . .' she struck her breast three times, then got up suddenly, carrying her bag, and peered into the confessionals hoping she might find a priest in one of them. 'It's too early, or it's not the day, but I'll come back,' she promised herself with tenderness. She lit the candle for Honora and went away feeling warm and quiet. She was blind and confused, too, and could not make up her mind what to do next. Where ever should she turn? It was a burning sin to spend money on taxicabs when there was always the hungry poor in the world, but she hailed one anyhow, and gave Honora's house number. Yes, there it was, just like in old times.

She read all the names pasted on slips above the bells, all the floors front and back, but Honora's name was not among them. The janitor had never heard of Mrs Terence Gogarty, nor Mrs Honora Gogarty, neither. Maybe it would be in the telephone book. There were many Gogartys but no Terence nor Honora. Rosaleen smothered down the impulse to tell the janitor, a good Irishman, how her dream had gone back on her. 'Thank ye kindly, it's no great matter,' she said, and stepped out into the street again. The wind hacked at her shoulders through the rag of a coat, the bag was too heavy altogether. Now what kind of nature was in Honora not to drop a line and say she had moved?

Walking about with her mind in a whirl, she came to a small dingy square with iron benches and some naked trees in it. Sitting, she began to shed tears again. When one handkerchief was wet she took out another, and the fresh perfume put new heart in her. She glanced around when a shadow fell on the corner of her eye, and there hunched on the other end of the bench was a scrap of a lad with freckles, his collar turned about his ears, his red hair wilted on his forehead under his bulging cap. He slanted his gooseberry eyes at her and said, 'We've all something to cry for in this world, isn't it so?'

Rosaleen said, 'I'm crying because I've come a long way for nothing.'

The boy said, 'I knew you was a County Sligo woman the minute I clapped eyes on ye.'

'God bless ye for that,' said Rosaleen, 'for I am.'

'I'm County Sligo myself, long ago, and curse the day I ever thought of leaving it,' said the boy, with such anger Rosaleen dried her eyes once for all and turned to have a good look at him.

'Whatever makes ye say that now?' she asked him. 'It's a good country, this. There's opportunity for all here.'

'So I've heard tell many's the countless times,' said the boy. 'There's all the opportunity in the wide world to shrivel with the hunger and walk the soles off your boots hunting the work, and there's a great chance of dying in the gutter at last. God forgive me the first thought I had of coming here.'

'Ye haven't been out long?' asked Rosaleen.

'Eleven months and five days the day,' said the boy. He plunged his hands into his pockets and stared at the freezing mud clotted around his luckless shoes.

'And what might ye do by way of a living?' asked Rosaleen.

'I'm an hostler,' he said. 'I used to work at the Dublin

race tracks, even. No man can tell me about horses,' he said proudly. 'And it's good work if it's to be found.'

Rosaleen looked attentively at his sharp red nose, frozen it was, and the stung look around his eyes, and the sharp bones sticking out at his wrists, and was surprised at herself for thinking, in the first glance, that he had the look of Kevin. She saw different now, but think if it had been Kevin! Better off to be dead and gone. 'I'm perishing of hunger and cold,' she told him, 'and if I knew where there was a place to eat, we'd have some lunch, for it's late.'

His eyes looked like he was drowning. 'Would ye? I know a place!' and he leaped up as if he meant to run. They did almost run to the edge of the square and the far corner. It was a Coffee Pot and full of the smell of hot cakes. 'We'll get our fill here,' said Rosaleen, taking off her gloves, 'though I'd never call it a grand place.'

The boy ate one thing after another as if he could never stop: roast beef and potatoes and spaghetti and custard pie and coffee, and Rosaleen ordered a package of cigarettes. It was like this with her, she was fond of the smell of tobacco, her husband was a famous smoker, never without his pipe. 'It's no use keeping it in,' said the boy. 'I haven't a penny, yesterday and today I didn't eat till now, and I've been fit to hang myself, or go to jail for a place to lay my head.'

Rosaleen said, 'I'm a woman doesn't have to think of money, I have all my heart desires, and a boy like yourself has a right to think nothing of a little loan will never be missed.' She fumbled in her purse and brought out a ten-dollar bill, crumpled it and pushed it under the rim of his saucer so the man behind the counter wouldn't notice. 'That's for luck in the new world,' she said, smiling at him. 'You might be Kevin or my own brother, or my own little lad alone in the world, and it'll surely come back to me if ever I need it.'

The boy said, 'I never thought to see this day,' and put the money in his pocket.

Rosaleen said, 'I don't even know your name, think of that!'

'I'm a blight on the name of Sullivan,' said he. 'Hugh it is – Hugh Sullivan.'

'That's a good enough name,' said Rosaleen. 'I've cousins named Sullivan in Dublin, but I never saw one of them. There was a man named Sullivan married my mother's sister, my aunt Brigid she was, and she went to live in Dublin. You're not related to the Dublin Sullivans, are ye?'

'I never heard of it, but maybe I am.'

'Ye have the look of a Sullivan to me,' said Rosaleen, 'and they're cousins of mine, some of them.' She ordered more coffee and he lit another cigarette, and she told him how she had come out more than twenty-five years past, a greenhorn like himself, and everything had turned out well for her and all her family here. Then she told about her husband, how he had been head waiter and a moneyed man, but he was old now; about the farm, if there was someone to help her, they could make a good thing of it; and about Kevin and the way he had gone away and died and sent her news of it in a dream; and this led to the dream about Honora, and here she was, the first time ever a dream had gone back on her. She went on to say there was always room for a strong willing boy in the country if he knew about horses, and how it was a shame for him to be tramping the streets with an empty stomach when there was everything to be had if he only knew which way to look for it. She leaned over and took him by the arm very urgently.

'You've a right to live in a good Irish house,' she told him. 'Why don't ye come home with me and live there like one of the family in peace and comfort?'

Hugh Sullivan stared at her out of his glazed green eyes down the edge of his sharp nose and a crafty look came over him. ' "Twould be dangerous,' he said. 'I'd hate to try it.'

'Dangerous, is it?' asked Rosaleen. 'What danger is there in the peaceful countryside?'

'It's not safe at all,' said Hugh. 'I was caught at it once

in Dublin, and there was a holy row! A fine woman like
yourself she was, and her husband peeking through a
crack in the wall the whole time. Man, that was a scrape
for ye!'

Rosaleen understood in her bones before her mind
grasped it. 'Whatever—' she began, and the blood boiled
up in her face until it was like looking through a red veil.
'Ye little whelp,' she said, trying to get her breath, 'so it's
that kind ye are, is it? I might know you're from Dublin!
Never in my whole life—' Her rage rose like a bonfire in
her, and she stopped. 'If I was looking for a man,' she
said, 'I'd choose a *man* and not a half-baked little . . .' She
took a deep breath and started again. 'The *cheek* of ye,'
she said, 'insulting a woman could be your mother. God
keep me from it! It's plain you're just an ignorant greenhorn, doesn't know the ways of decent people, and now
be off—' She stood up and motioned to the man behind
the counter. 'Out of that door now—'

He stood up too, glancing around fearfully with his
narrow green eyes, and put out a hand as if he would try
to make it up with her. 'Not so loud now, woman alive,
it's what any man might think the way ye're—'

Rosaleen said, 'Hold your tongue or I'll tear it out of
your head!' and her right arm went back in a business-
like way.

He ducked and shot past her, then collected himself

45

and lounged out of reach. 'Farewell to ye, County Sligo woman,' he said tauntingly. 'I'm from County Cork myself!' and darted through the door.

Rosaleen shook so she could hardly find the money for the bill, and she couldn't see her way before her, but when the cold air struck her, her head cleared, and she could have almost put a curse on Honora for making all this trouble for her . . .

She took a train the short way home, for the taste of travel had soured on her altogether. She wanted to be home and nowhere else. That shameless boy, whatever was he thinking of? 'Boys do be known for having evil minds in them,' she told herself, and the blood fairly crinkled in her veins. But he had said, 'A fine woman like yourself,' and maybe he'd met too many bold ones, and thought they were all alike; maybe she had been too free in her ways because he was Irish and looked so sad and poor. But there it was, he was a mean sort, and he would have made love to her if she hadn't stopped him, maybe. It flashed over her and she saw it clear as day – Kevin had loved her all the time, and she had sent him away to that cheap girl who wasn't half good enough for him! And Kevin a sweet decent boy would have cut off his right hand rather than give her an improper word. Kevin had loved her and she had loved Kevin and, oh, she hadn't known it in time! She bowed herself back into the corner with her elbow on the window-sill, her old fur collar pulled up around her face, and wept long and bitterly for Kevin, who would have stayed if she had said the word – and now he was gone and lost and dead. She would hide herself from the world and never speak to a soul again.

'Safe and sound she is, Dennis,' Rosaleen told him. 'She's been dangerous, but it's past. I left her in health.'

'That's good enough,' said Dennis, without enthusiasm. He took off his cap with the ear flaps and ran his fingers through his downy white hair and put the cap on again and stood waiting to hear the wonders of the trip; but Rosaleen had no tales to tell and was full of homecoming.

'This kitchen is a disgrace,' she said, putting things to rights. 'But not for all the world would I live in the city, Dennis. It's a wild heartless place, full of criminals in every direction as far as the eye can reach. I was scared for my life the whole time. Light the lamp, will you?'

The native boy sat warming his great feet in the oven, and his teeth were chattering with something more than cold. He burst out: 'I seed sumpin' comin' up the road whiles ago. Black. Fust it went on all fours like a dawg and then it riz and walked longside of me on its hind legs. I was scairt, I was. I said Shoo! at it, and it went out, like a lamp.'

'Maybe it was a dog,' said Dennis.

''Twarn't a dawg, neither,' said the boy.

'Maybe 'twas a cat rising up to climb a fence,' said Rosaleen.

''Twarn't a cat, neither,' said the boy. ''Twarn't nothin' I ever seed afore, nor *you*, neither.'

'Never you mind about that,' said Rosaleen. 'I have seen it and many times, when I was a girl in Ireland. It's famous there, the way it comes in a black lump and rolls along the path before you, but if you call on the Holy Name and make the sign of the Cross, it flees away. Eat your supper now, and sleep here the night; ye can't go out by your lone and the Evil waiting for ye.'

She bedded him down in Kevin's room, and kept Dennis awake all hours telling him about the ghosts she'd seen in Sligo. The trip to Boston seemed to have gone out of her mind entirely.

In the morning, the boy's starveling black dog rose up at the opened kitchen door and stared sorrowfully at his master. The cats streamed out in a body, and silently, intently they chased him far up the road. The boy stood on the doorstep and began to tremble again. 'The old woman told me to git back fer supper,' he said blankly. 'Howma *ever* gointa git back fer supper *now*? The ole man'll skin me alive.'

Rosaleen wrapped her green wool shawl around her

head and shoulders. 'I'll go along with ye and tell what happened,' she said. 'They'll never harm ye when they know the straight of it.' For he was shaking with fright until his knees buckled under him. 'He's away in his mind,' she thought, with pity. 'Why can't they see it and let him be in peace?'

The steady slope of the lane ran on for nearly a mile, then turned into a bumpy trail leading to a forlorn house with broken-down steps and a litter of rubbish around them. The boy hung back more and more, and stopped short when the haggard, long-toothed woman in the gray dress came out carrying a stick of stove wood. The woman stopped short too when she recognized Rosaleen, and a sly cold look came on her face.

'Good day,' said Rosaleen. 'Your boy saw a ghost last night, and I didn't have the heart to send him out in the darkness. He slept safe in my house.'

The woman gave a sharp dry bark, like a fox. 'Ghosts!' she said. 'From all I hear, there's more than ghosts around your house nights, Missis O'Toole.' She wagged her head and her faded tan hair flew in strings. 'A pretty specimen you are, Missis O'Toole, with your old husband and the young boys in your house and the traveling salesmen and the drunkards lolling on your doorstep all hours—'

'Hold your tongue before your lad here,' said Rosaleen, the back of her neck beginning to crinkle. She was so taken by surprise she couldn't find a ready answer, but stood in her tracks listening.

'A pretty sight you are, Missis O'Toole,' said the woman, raising her thin voice somewhat, but speaking with deadly cold slowness. 'With your trips away from your husband and your loud-colored dresses and your dyed hair—'

'May God strike you dead,' said Rosaleen, raising her own voice suddenly, 'if you say that of my hair! And for the rest may your evil tongue rot in your head with your teeth! I'll not waste words on ye! Here's your poor lad and may God pity him in your house, a blight on it! And if my own house is burnt over my head I'll know who did it!' She turned away and whirled back to call out, 'May ye be ten years dying!'

'You can curse and swear, Missis O'Toole, but the whole countryside knows about you!' cried the other, brandishing her stick like a spear.

'Much good they'll get of it!' shouted Rosaleen, striding away in a roaring fury. 'Dyed, is it?' She raised her clenched fist and shook it at the world. 'Oh, the liar!' and her rage was like a drum beating time for her marching legs. What was happening these days that everybody she met had dirty minds and dirty tongues in their heads? Oh, why wasn't she strong enough to strangle them all at once? Her eyes were so hot she couldn't close her lids over them. She went on staring and walking, until almost before she knew it she came in sight of her own house, sitting like a hen quietly in a nest of snow. She slowed down, her thumping heart eased a little, and she sat on a stone by the roadside to catch her breath and gather her wits before she must see Dennis. As she sat, it came to her that the Evil walking the roads at night in this place was the bitter lies people had been telling about her, who had been a good woman all this time when many another would have gone astray. It was no comfort now to remember all the times she might have done wrong and hadn't. What was the good if she was being scandalized all the same? That lad in Boston now – the little whelp. She spat on the frozen earth and wiped her mouth. Then she put her elbows on her knees and her head in her hands, and thought, 'So that's the way it is here, is it? That's what my life has come to, I'm a woman of bad fame with the neighbors.'

Dwelling on this strange thought, little by little she began to feel better. Jealousy, of course, that was it. 'Ah, what wouldn't that poor thing give to have my hair?' and she patted it tenderly. From the beginning it had been so, the women were jealous, because the men were everywhere after her, as if it was her fault! Well, let them talk. Let them. She knew in her heart what she was, and Dennis knew, and that was enough.

'Life is a dream,' she said aloud, in a soft easy melancholy. 'It's a mere dream.' The thought and the words pleased her, and she gazed with pleasure at the loosened stones of the wall across the road, dark brown, with the thin shining coat of ice on them, in a comfortable daze until her feet began to feel chilled.

'Let me not sit here and take my death at my early time of life,' she cautioned herself, getting up and wrapping her shawl carefully around her. She was thinking how this sad countryside needed some young hearts in it, and how she wished Kevin would come back to laugh with her at that woman up the hill; with him, she could just laugh in their faces! That dream about Honora now, it hadn't come true at all. Maybe the dream about Kevin wasn't true either. If one dream failed on you it would be foolish to think another mightn't fail you too: wouldn't it, wouldn't it? She smiled at Dennis sitting by the stove.

'What did the native people have to say this morning?' he asked, trying to pretend it was nothing much to him what they said.

'Oh, we exchanged the compliments of the season,' said Rosaleen. 'There was no call for more.' She went about singing; her heart felt light as a leaf and she couldn't have told why if she died for it. But she was a good woman and she'd show them she was going to be one to her last day. Ah, she'd show them, the low-minded things.

In the evening they settled down by the stove, Dennis cleaning and greasing his boots, Rosaleen with the long tablecloth she'd been working on for fifteen years. Dennis kept wondering what had happened in Boston, or where ever she had been. He knew he would never hear the straight of it, but he wanted Rosaleen's story about it. And there she sat mum, putting a lot of useless stitches in something she would never use, even if she ever finished it, which she would not.

'Dennis,' she said after a while, 'I don't put the respect on dreams I once did.'

'That's maybe a good thing,' said Dennis, cautiously. 'And why don't you?'

'All day long I've been thinking Kevin isn't dead at all, and we shall see him in this very house before long.'

Dennis growled in his throat a little. 'That's no sign at all,' he said. And to show that he had a grudge against her he laid down his meerschaum pipe, stuffed his old briar and lit it instead. Rosaleen took no notice at all. Her embroidery had fallen on her knees and she was listening to the rattle and clatter of a buggy coming down the road, with Richards's voice roaring a song, 'I've been working on the *railroad*, ALL the live-long day!' She stood up, taking hairpins out and putting them back, her hands trembling. Then she ran to the looking-glass and saw her face there, leaping into shapes fit to scare you.

'Oh, Dennis,' she cried out as if it was that thought had driven her out of her chair. 'I forgot to buy a looking-glass, I forgot it altogether!'

'It's a good enough glass,' repeated Dennis.

The buggy clattered at the gate, the song halted. Ah, he was coming in, surely! It flashed through her mind a woman would have a ruined life with such a man, it was courting death and danger to let him set foot over the threshold.

She stopped herself from running to the door, hand on the knob even before his knock should sound. Then the wheels creaked and ground again, the song started up; if he thought of stopping he changed his mind and went on, off on his career to the Saturday night dance in Winston, with his rapscallion cronies.

Rosaleen didn't know what to expect, then, and then: surely he couldn't be stopping? Ah, surely he *couldn't* be going on? She sat down again with her heart just nowhere, and took up the tablecloth, but for a long time she couldn't see the stitches. She was wondering what had become of her life; every day she had thought something great was going to happen, and it was all just straying from one terrible disappointment to another. Here in the lamplight sat Dennis and the cats, beyond in the darkness and snow lay Winston and New York and Boston, and beyond that were far-off places full of life and gayety she'd never seen nor even heard of, and beyond everything like a green field with morning sun on it lay youth and Ireland as if they were something she had dreamed, or made up in a story. Ah, what was there to remember, or to look forward to now? Without thinking at all, she leaned over and put her head on Dennis's knee. 'Whyever,' she asked him, in an ordinary voice, 'did ye marry a woman like me?'

'Mind you don't tip over in that chair now,' said Dennis. 'I knew well I could never do better.' His bosom began to thaw and simmer. It was going to be all right with everything, he could see that.

She sat up and felt his sleeves carefully. 'I want you to wrap up warm this bitter weather, Dennis,' she told him. 'With two pairs of socks and the chest protector, for if anything happened to you whatever would become of me in this world?'

'Let's not think of it,' said Dennis, shuffling his feet.

'Let's not, then,' said Rosaleen. 'For I could cry if you crooked a finger at me.'